The HOME Team
Nashville Predators®

Written by Holly Preston
Illustrated by James Hearne

Always Books Ltd.

The Home Team™: Nashville Predators®

Manufactured by Friesens Corporation in Altona, MB, Canada
April 2018
Job #242047

ISBN 978-0-9938974-3-6 (pbk.)

Editing by Visible Ink Incorporated

Layout by James Hearne

Always Books Ltd.

AFANFORLIFE.COM™

For all young PREDATORS® fans
who know there's no team like ours!

There was nothing better than playing hockey ...

... except watching hockey when the NASHVILLE PREDATORS played.

William played forward. Elijah played defense. James was in goal.
The boys played different positions. They had the same dream:
to one day play for the NASHVILLE PREDATORS.

Even after playing all day, William dreamed only about hockey.

The only problem was William never scored. Ever.
The puck went high. The puck went low.
The puck went everywhere but where it was supposed to go.

How can I ever play for the PREDATORS? William wondered.
His sister Emma was the best goal scorer in the neighborhood.

"The PREDATORS were little boys once, too, William," his dad said.
"They didn't become hockey stars overnight."

His mom said, "You can learn a lot by watching what the PREDATORS do."
She'd been a PREDATORS fan forever.

The PREDATORS are great skaters.

They make big plays.

They shoot. They score!

And make a million saves.

"The only way to get better is to practice," said Elijah.
And so they practiced hard. And then came the best suprise they'd ever had.
"We're going to a PREDATORS game!" James yelled.

But at the game, the PREDATORS' top scorer wasn't scoring at all!
"Something is wrong," said William.

The next day on the way to the rink, William found a shiny chain.
He put it on and ... he got a goal! And then another one!
"That's a good luck charm, for sure," Emma said.

"Our player lost his good luck charm, kids," said Dad. "Maybe *that's* why he hasn't been scoring." The children knew hockey players were superstitious. They also knew where the charm was ...

... and what they had to do next!

William seized the moment.
"What does it take to play for the NASHVILLE PREDATORS?" he asked.

Play like a team ...

... and with heart.

Never give up.

Believe in yourself.

"The PREDATORS are the greatest team in the NHL," said Elijah.
"We're going to be PREDATORS fans forever," added James.

Everything was the way it should be.

All the next week William practiced and practiced.
He no longer had the good luck charm, but he had something else —
he believed in himself.

And that was all he really needed.

But William, like all hockey players, knew a little luck always helps ...

... especially when you're playing for the Stanley Cup®!

ABOUT THE AUTHOR

Holly Preston

Holly grew up watching NHL hockey with her brother and father. Now she creates children's picture books for professional sports teams. She hopes Predators fans will enjoy having a book that celebrates their home team and encourages young fans to find a love of reading.

ABOUT THE ILLUSTRATOR

James Hearne

Born in London, England, James began his art career at the tender age of eight, selling drawings to guests at his grandparents' hotel. He continues to sell his whimsical illustrations around the globe as a full-time illustrator and full-time hockey fan.